CHANGING HABITS, LIVING GREEN

BY DARLENE R. STILLE

The Child's World

Published by The Child's World®
1980 Lookout Drive • Mankato, MN 56003-1705
800-599-READ • www.childsworld.com

PHOTO CREDITS
Diego Cervo/Shutterstock Images, cover, 1; Morgan Lane Photography/
Shutterstock Images, 5; Shutterstock Images, 7, 13, 27; James Brey/
iStockphoto, 9; Fotolia, 11, 23; Marilyn Nieves/iStockphoto, 15;
Rob Friedman/iStockphoto, 17; Melissa Madia/iStockphoto, 19;
Catherine Yeulet/iStockphoto, 21; Kim Gunkel/iStockphoto, 25;
Grady Reese/Shutterstock Images, 29

CONTENT CONSULTANT
Karen O'Connor, co-owner, Mother Earth Gardens,
Minneapolis, Minnesota

ACKNOWLEDGMENTS
The Child's World®: Mary Berendes, Publishing Director
The Design Lab: Design
Red Line Editorial: Editorial direction

ISBN: 978-1-60973-169-4
LCCN: 2011927665

Printed in the United States of America in Mankato, MN
July, 2011
PA02090

TABLE OF CONTENTS

You Can Help Earth, 4

Tips for Going Green, 6

More Ways to Go Green, 30

Words to Know, 31

Further Reading, 32

Index, 32

YOU CAN HELP EARTH

Earth has limited resources for much of what we use every day. There is only so much drinking water, **fossil fuels**, and farmland. People are using more of these valuable resources. Some resources are renewable, like trees. This means they can be replaced after being used. However, too many forests are being cut down and not replaced.

Using up resources also pollutes air. Burning fossil fuels contributes to air pollution and **global warming**. Because Earth is warming, polar ice caps are melting. This is destroying **habitats** of many animals.

There are many ways to "go green." Recycle more and use fewer things to help protect Earth.

What can be done? Many people think we must "go green." Going green is a way of living that is friendly to Earth. It means using fewer resources to keep Earth clean. It means burning less fossil fuel. It means using fewer things and recycling more. Going green starts with you. There are many things you can do each day to help the environment!

TURN OFF THE WATER!

Turn off the water while you brush your teeth. You really only need to turn on the faucet to wet your brush and to rinse your mouth and the sink. Leaving the water running while you brush could use up to eight gallons (30 L) of water a day!

WHY?

Before water comes through the faucet, it must go through treatment plants to be cleaned. Treating water uses energy. To make energy, we must use limited resources such as fossil fuels. Turning off the water while you brush saves more than 200 gallons (757 L) a month from being cleaned in a treatment plant.

Turn off the faucet while you brush your teeth to save water.

TIME YOUR SHOWER

Do you take a bath to get clean? Filling a bathtub can use up to 70 gallons (265 L) of water. Taking a shower only uses 10 to 25 gallons (38–95 L). The quicker you shower, the less water you use. Take a timer into the shower with you. See if you can get in and out in five minutes or less.

WHY?

Suppose every person in the United States used one less gallon of water in the shower every day. The savings at the end of the year would be 85 billion gallons (322 billion L) of water. The water then does not need to be treated again at a treatment plant. Fewer fossil fuels are used in treatment plants, and less pollution goes into the air.

CLEAR

RESET

HOUR

MIN

Try to shower for only five minutes. You will save many gallons of water per year.

GET RECHARGED!

Your toy stopped working. The batteries are dead! Instead of grabbing new disposable batteries, go for rechargeable ones. All you need are a few rechargeable batteries and a charger. You can recharge these batteries hundreds of times. For each rechargeable battery you use, you save hundreds of regular batteries from the garbage.

WHY?

Most batteries contain mercury. It is a very poisonous liquid. If batteries are thrown in the trash, they end up in a landfill. Over time, the mercury leaks out and pollutes groundwater. Instead, save up your old batteries and take them to a recycling center.

Create less trash by using rechargeable batteries.

NO TRASH DAY!

For one day each week, throw as little into the garbage as you can. After you have recycled cans, bottles, and paper, make **compost** out of leftover vegetables. Compost is a mixture of old food scraps and plants that becomes fertilizer. Most important, try to **reduce** how much stuff you use. The fewer things you use, the less garbage you'll make.

WHY?

Most household garbage goes into landfills. Each person in the United States makes almost 4.5 pounds (2 kg) of trash every day. That adds up to 250 million tons (227 million t) of garbage dumped into landfills every year! The garbage leaks methane, a **greenhouse gas**.

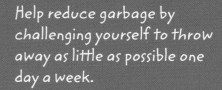

Help reduce garbage by challenging yourself to throw away as little as possible one day a week.

TRASH IT NATION

Students at the Guajome Park Academy in Vista, California, saw a chance to go green. Their school is located in a wetlands preserve area. In 2009, the students formed a team to clean up the school grounds and the wetlands. The team picked up candy wrappers, plastic bottles, fast food wrappers, and other garbage in the wetlands. They recycled plastic, glass, cardboard, and paper.

BE GREEN ON THE GO

Instead of asking grown-ups to drive you somewhere in a car, get in the habit of walking. You could also ride your bike. You'll help slow down or stop global warming.

WHY?

Most cars burn gasoline, which sends carbon dioxide into Earth's atmosphere. Carbon dioxide is the main greenhouse gas that causes global warming. The Environmental Protection Agency estimates that the average family car gives off 11,450 pounds (5,194 kg) of carbon dioxide each year. Drive less and decrease your contribution of carbon dioxide into the air.

Biking to places is a habit that is good for the environment.

BE AN ENERGY STAR

Help keep your refrigerator running like a star. Decide what you need from the fridge before you open the door. Never leave the door open while you spread butter on your toast or use other foods from the fridge.

WHY?

Keeping the door closed means the refrigerator doesn't have to work as hard to keep cold. It uses less electricity. The power plant then burns less fossil fuel. Burning less fossil fuel means less greenhouse gases in the atmosphere to cause global warming.

Decide what you need before you open the refrigerator door so you can close it quickly.

DONATE YOUR GIFT

Do you have a birthday coming up? Ask friends and family to pool their gift money. Ask them not to buy that new video game or book you wanted. Instead, ask them to donate the money to a **conservation** group in your name.

WHY?

There are many conservation and environmental groups in the United States. The Sierra Club is devoted to saving wilderness areas. The World Wildlife Fund focuses on protecting animals. There are even groups that direct their efforts toward oceans or wetlands. These groups work to pass laws that help protect nature.

Environmental groups conserve wetlands, which are home to many animals.

THE GREAT OUTDOORS

Instead of coming home from school and playing
a video game with some friends, head outdoors.
Take a bat and baseball. Jump rope, play tag,
or ride your bike around the neighborhood.
You save the energy it takes to watch television
or play on the computer. Plus, you get some
exercise and fresh air!

WHY?

It takes a lot of energy for video games to work.
A study by the National Resources Defense
Council found that all the US home video game
systems used as much electricity every year as
the entire city of San Diego, California.

Playing tag outside instead of watching television or using the computer saves energy.

TIP #9

USE SMART PLUG STRIPS

Use a smart plug strip to turn all your stuff off at once. Smart plug strips sense when you are not using your computer, printer, or anything else that you plug into the strip. When these devices are not being used, the smart strip cuts off the small amount of energy that still flows to them.

WHY?

Even when they are turned off, computers, televisions, and printers use energy. The energy is nicknamed vampire power. Vampire power makes up 10 percent of electricity used by US homes and offices. Power plants that make this electricity often burn fossil fuels. So, less vampire power means less global warming!

Save energy by using a smart plug strip that can cut off vampire power.

10

DO YOU REALLY NEED THAT?

You've heard of the three Rs: reduce, reuse, and recycle! The first thing you can do to go green is reduce. This means use and buy less stuff. When you're about to buy something, ask yourself if you really need it. Do you really need that new shirt? Instead of buying it, have a clothing exchange with your friends. Everyone will bring a couple things they don't wear anymore. It's reducing and reusing shopping!

WHY?

By reducing how much you buy, you are helping Earth. How? New things are made in factories that usually burn fossil fuels. Buying less stuff means you're contributing less to burning fossil fuels and to global warming!

Gather together the clothes you don't wear anymore. Then have a clothing exchange with your friends.

25

LESS PACKAGING, PLEASE!

You've heard you should bring a reusable bag to the grocery store. But you can also buy foods that have less packaging. The items the store clerk puts into your bag are likely wrapped in another layer of plastic. Ask the grown-ups in your home to buy in bulk. Large containers of milk, juice, chips, or other food can be put into smaller reusable containers at home. Also, fresh foods on the outer edge of the store usually have less packaging than the foods in the middle aisles.

WHY?

Of all the garbage thrown away by the average family, packaging accounts for about 65 percent. You help reduce trash by buying items that have less plastic or paper packaging to throw away.

Buy food in bulk and store in
smaller reusable containers.
This reduces how much
packaging you throw away.

TIP #12

SPREAD THE WORD

Have your class start a go green project. Each of your classmates could make a poster about their favorite way to go green. Ask local businesses to hang up your posters. Your teacher can help you get your posters on display.

WHY?

Kids can play an important role in spreading the word about going green. Big changes often start with one person. And that person is you!

> Spread the word about going green by getting your class to make posters about green habits.

IT STARTS WITH ONE

Nine-year-old Melissa Poe was upset by a television program that showed Earth in the future as a dying planet. In the 1990s, she and six friends formed Kids for a Clean Environment. Her work caught people's attention. Other kids began to form chapters of her group. The organization grew to more than 2,000 chapters with 300,000 kids working to save energy and habitats.

29

MORE WAYS TO GO GREEN

1. **Throw** facial tissue in the trash instead of flushing it. If all the people in the United States flushed the toilet just one less time per day, the water saved would fill a lake one mile long, one mile wide, and four feet deep.

2. **Pick** the right time of day to help with watering the lawn or garden. The best time is early in the morning or late in the evening when it is cool and less water will evaporate.

3. **Talk** to your parents about getting a rain barrel. Then you can use rainwater to water the garden and indoor plants.

4. **Keep** cold water in a pitcher in the refrigerator instead of running the tap to get cool water.

5. **Reuse** old sauce or ketchup bottles in craft projects. You can make vases by wrapping them with scraps of colored paper and string.

6. **After** a picnic lunch, wash plastic glasses, silverware, and plates. Use them on another picnic.

7. **Find** out about Earth Day activities in your community and join in.

8. **Organize** your classmates to write letters to the publishers of the textbooks that you use. Request that they print their future books on recycled paper. Or, ask them to make e-books!

9. **Turn** off the lights whenever you leave a room that is not being used.

10. **Close** the door to your home to hold in heat during winter or keep it cool during summer.

11. **Be** sure the dishwasher is full before you run a load of dishes.

12. **Choose** toys and games that are well made and will last a long time. Look for toys made of wood or recycled materials.

WORDS TO KNOW

compost (KOM-pohst): Compost is a mixture of leaves, old food scraps, and soil that is used to fertilize plants and land. Making compost helps reduce food garbage.

conservation (kon-sur-VAY-shun): Conservation is the preservation of the natural world. Organizations around the world are involved in conservation of different types of land.

fossil fuels (FOSS-ul FYOO-uls): Fossil fuels are oil, natural gas, and coal, which formed from the remains of ancient plants. Burning fossil fuels leads to global warming.

global warming (GLOHB-ul WOR-ming): Global warming is the heating up of Earth's atmosphere and oceans due to air pollution. You can change your habits to help slow down or stop global warming.

greenhouse gas (GREEN-houss GASS): A greenhouse gas is a gas like carbon dioxide or methane that helps hold heat in the atmosphere. Too much greenhouse gas in the atmosphere leads to global warming.

habitats (HAB-uh-tats): Habitats are the natural homes of animals or other living things. Many habitats need to be protected.

reduce (ree-DOOS): To reduce means to make smaller or less in amount or size. A simple way to help Earth is to reduce how much stuff you use.

FURTHER READING

BOOKS

Chamber, Catherine. *Go Green! Lead the Way*, New York: Crabtree Publishing, 2010.

O'Ryan, Ellie. *Easy to Be Green*. New York: Simon & Schuster, 2009.

Roca, Núria. *The Three R's: Reuse, Reduce, Recycle*. Hauppauge, NY: Barron's Educational Series, 2007.

WEB SITES

Visit our Web site for links about changing habits and living green:
http://www.childsworld.com/links

Note to Parents, Teachers, and Librarians: We routinely verify our Web links to make sure they are safe and active sites. So encourage your readers to check them out!

animals, 4, 18

biking, 14, 20

carbon dioxide, 14

compost, 12

conservation, 18

energy, 6, 16, 20, 22, 29

fossil fuels, 4, 5, 6, 8, 16, 22, 24

garbage, 10, 12, 13, 26

global warming, 4, 14, 16, 22, 24

playing, 20

reducing, 5, 12, 24, 26

water, 4, 6, 8, 10